Down on the Farm

PIGS

Hannah Ray

QED Publishing

First published in the UK in 2006 by
QED Publishing
A Quarto Group company
226 City Road
London EC1V 2TT
www.qed-publishing.co.uk

A Catalogue record for this book is available from
the British Library.

ISBN 1 84538 356 7

Written by Hannah Ray
Designed by Liz Wiffen
Consultant Sally Morgan
Editor Paul Manning
Picture Researcher Joanne Forrest Smith
Illustrations by Chris Davidson

Publisher Steve Evans
Editorial Director Jean Coppendale
Art Director Zeta Davies

Printed and bound in China

Picture credits

Key: t = top, b = bottom, c = centre,
l = left, r = right, FC = front cover

Alamy /Penny Boyd 7, /David Hoffman Photo Library
5, /Holt Studios/Sarah Rowland 17T, /Renee Morris 4,
11; **Corbis** /Claro Cortes IV 19, /Robert Dowling 16T,
/Owen Franken 15B, /Peter Worth 9; **FLPA** /Jurgen &
Christine Sohns 16B; **Getty Images** /Peter Cade 8B,
/Robert Daly 14, /Bob Elsdale 13, 22, /Bill Ling 6,
/Thorsten Milse FC, 1, 8T, /Antony Nagelmann 10,
/Ryan Pierse 18, /Robert Ross 17B, /Andy Sacks 12.

CONTENTS

Words in **bold** can be found in the Glossary on page 22.

Pigs on the farm

Do you know where ham and bacon come from? Or the pork sausages that you cook on the barbecue? What about the **bristles** in your paintbrush? All these things come from pigs.

Farmers all over the world keep pigs. Pigs give us lots of different types of meat. They are found everywhere except Antarctica.

Pigs from nose to tail

A fully grown pig is about 80cm tall at the shoulder and weighs about 90kg. That's the same weight as four and a half six-year-old children!

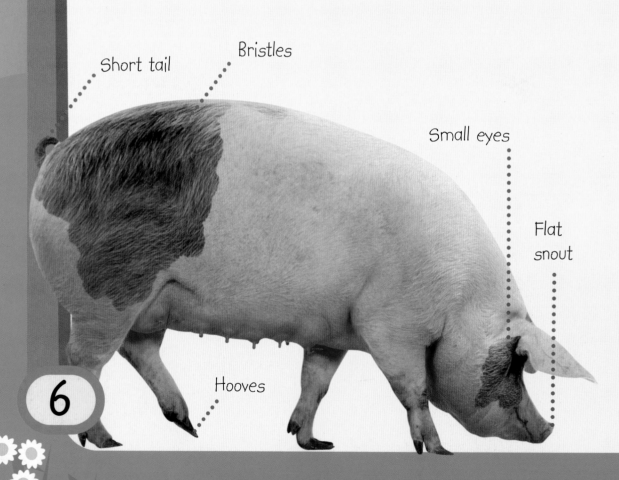

Short tail

Bristles

Small eyes

Flat snout

Hooves

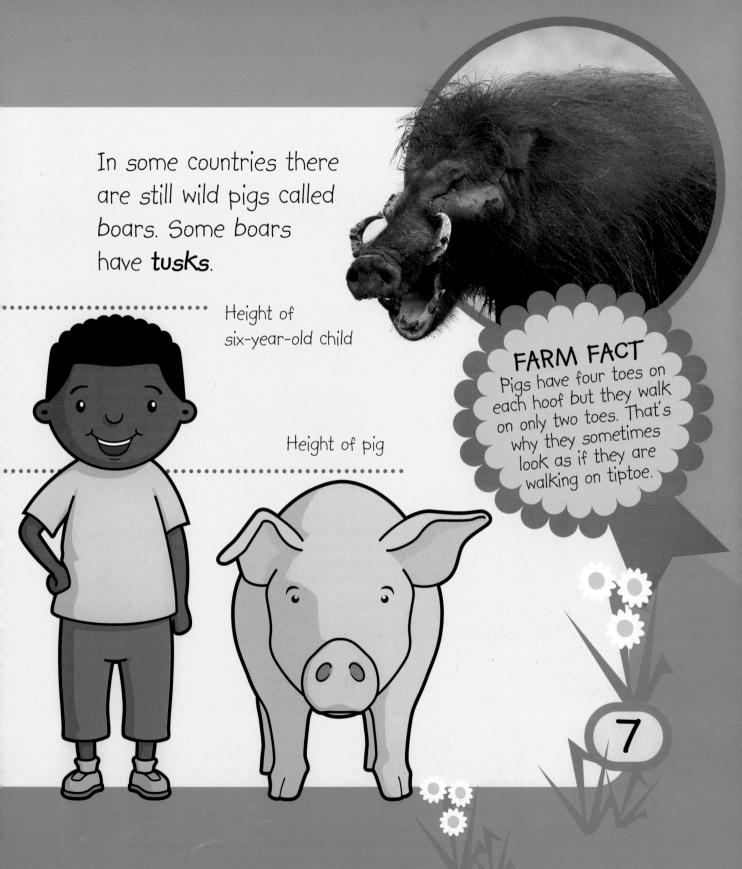

In some countries there are still wild pigs called boars. Some boars have **tusks**.

Height of six-year-old child

Height of pig

FARM FACT

Pigs have four toes on each hoof but they walk on only two toes. That's why they sometimes look as if they are walking on tiptoe.

7

It's a pig's life...

A baby pig is called a piglet. Before a piglet is born, it grows inside its mother for 16 weeks. The mother pig, or sow, can give birth to about 18 piglets in one **litter**.

For the first few weeks, the piglets feed on their mother's milk.

A mother pig feeding her babies.

These Saddleback piglets are about 14 weeks old.

At two weeks old, the piglets start to eat other food too, such as **cereals**, plants and vegetable scraps.

At seven months, a female pig is big enough to have babies of her own. Sows usually give birth to two litters every year.

On a farm, pigs live for 10 to 15 years.

9

Big bad pig?

Many people think that pigs are smelly, dirty and not very clever, but this is not true.

Pigs are very clever. In fact, they are more intelligent than dogs and cats.

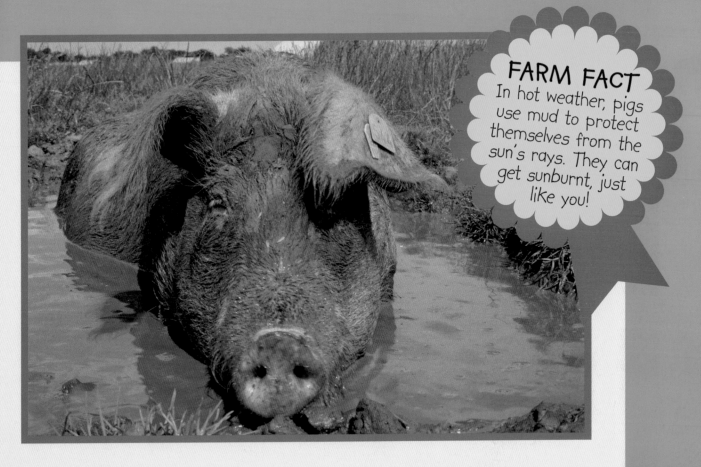

FARM FACT
In hot weather, pigs use mud to protect themselves from the sun's rays. They can get sunburnt, just like you!

Pigs do not roll in mud because they like being dirty. They do it to cool down because they cannot **sweat**.

Pigs keep their **nest** very clean. They go to the toilet as far away as possible from where they sleep.

11

Piggy pals

Pigs are very friendly. They can use up to 20 different noises to speak to each other.

Newborn piglets will run to their mother when she calls them. When the piglets are only five to ten days old, their mother encourages them to leave the nest to meet other pigs.

12

Piglets are very playful animals.
They enjoy play-fighting and
throwing things up
in the air, just
for fun!

FARM FACT
Sows 'sing' to their
piglets while they
feed them.

13

From pork to paintbrushes

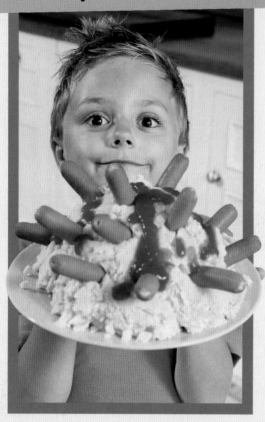

Pigs are kept mainly for their meat, but they give us other things, too. Leather called pigskin is used to make gloves, wallets, handbags and belts.

Pigs give us sausages, bacon, ham and pork.

In some countries, such as France, pigs are used to find rare wild **fungi** called truffles, which grow underground. The pigs use their amazing sense of smell to hunt out the truffles and dig them up with their snouts.

14

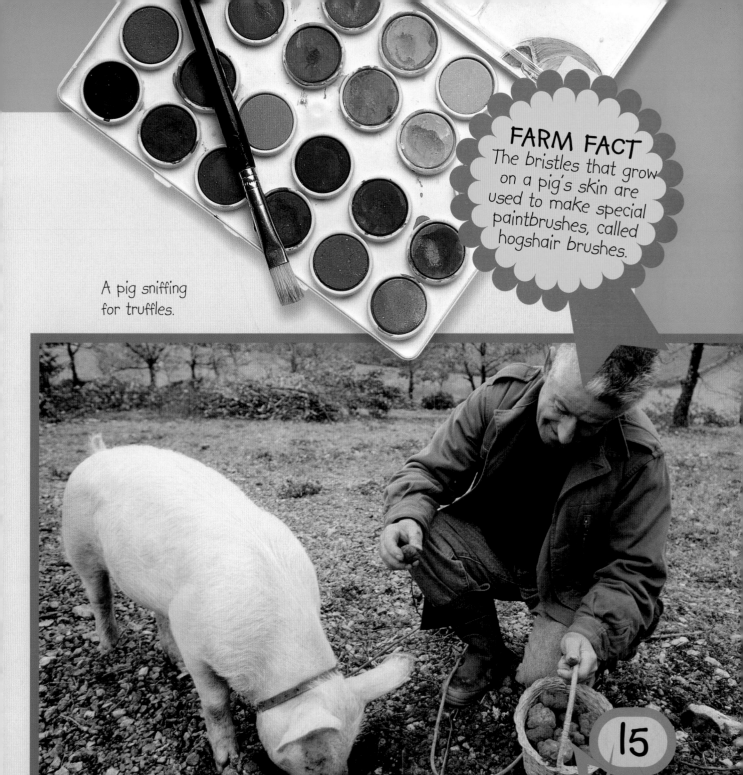

A pig sniffing for truffles.

15

Pigs around the world

MIDDLE WHITE

These funny-faced pigs are from Yorkshire. They are very good-natured and talkative.

SWABIAN HALL SWINE

These pigs come from Germany and they are famous for their meat. They can be recognized by their black heads and black tails.

FARM FACT
The smallest pig is the Pygmy Hog. Males are 65cm long, 25cm tall and weigh 8–9kg.

GLOUCESTER OLD SPOT

These large pigs are an old English breed. They were once called '**orchard pigs**' because they ate the apples that fell to the ground in apple orchards.

RED RIVER HOG

These unusual wild pigs live in western and central Africa. They rest during the day and are active at night.

17

Piggy customs

FRANCE

Every August in a town in the South of France, the people celebrate everything piggy. There is a prize for the best pig costume, a piglet race and even a pig **imitation** contest!

Piglet racing in the South of France.

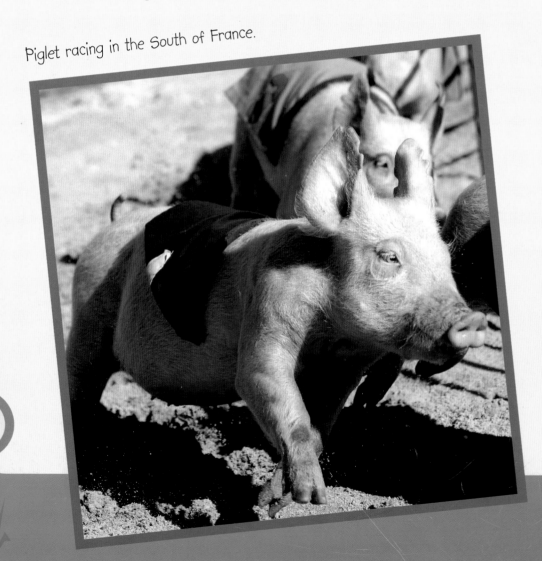

PHILIPPINES

In June every year, roasted pigs are carried through towns in the Philippines and are eaten at a big party. The roasted pigs are called 'lechons'.

CHINA

In China, each year is named after one of twelve animals. People born in the Chinese Year of the Pig always tell the truth and are good friends. They try their best at everything.

FARM FACT
Pigs can swim! In America, a pig called Priscilla is even said to have saved a small boy from drowning!

19

Make a piggy bank

To make this fun piggy bank you will need lots of strips of newspaper, some wallpaper paste, a balloon, an egg carton, a pipe cleaner, some sticky tape, a marker pen and lots of pink paint.

1 Blow up the balloon. Stick on three or four complete layers of newspaper strips using lots of wallpaper paste.

2 Let the layers dry out overnight. Then pop the balloon and remove it. You now have your piggy body.

3 With sticky tape, stick on four egg-carton legs, an egg-carton snout and two flaps of card for the ears.

BRIGHT IDEA
Your pig does not have to be pink. Why not try making it spotty, stripy or even painting big, bright flowers all over it!

4 Bend the pipe cleaner into a curly tail and stick it on with sticky tape.

5 Paint your pig and let it dry. Then draw on eyes and a big smile.

6 Ask a grown-up to cut a slot in the top of your pig, so that you can put money into your piggy bank.

21

Glossary and Index

bristle thick hair that grows on a pig's skin, used to make paintbrushes

cereal food grains such as wheat, barley or rye

fungi mushrooms, toadstools and truffles that grow wild in woods and fields

imitation copying, or pretending to be, something or someone

litter a number of baby pigs that are all born at one time

nest area where a pig sleeps, often a pile of straw

orchard field where fruit trees grow

sweat when our skin becomes damp to help us cool down

tusk long, pointed tooth on a boar or elephant

22

Ideas for teachers and parents

- Make a pig poster. Take a large sheet of paper and draw the outline of a pig. Look through comics, magazines and newspapers and cut out anything pig-related. Look out for scraps of pink material, buttons or ribbons. Collect your bits and pieces and use them to fill in the pig outline.

- Research different breeds of pig and make factsheets comparing the children's favourite breeds.

- Visit a children's farm so the children can see real pigs.

- Help the children make a list of all the stories they know that feature pigs, for example, "The Three Little Pigs".

- Find poems about pigs and help the children make up a funny pig poem of their own. Use lots of words beginning with the letter 'p'. Try writing your poem in a pig shape.

- Have fun making piggy noises with the children. Who can snort the loudest?

- Make a simple wordsearch for the children using pig-related vocabulary from this book.

- Make a thumbprint pig picture. Help the children to draw a farmyard scene on a large sheet of paper and make thumbprints around the farmyard using pink fingerpaints. When the pink paint has dried, use a marker pen to add legs, a curly tail, a snout, eyes and a big smile to each 'pig'.

- Make a pig mask out of a paper plate. Paint the plate pink and cut out eyeholes. Cut out a pair of floppy ears from pink felt and stick them to the mask. Add an egg-carton nose and draw on a piggy smile. Add holes to each side of the mask and tie on a piece of elastic so the mask can be worn.